Starring Grace

For Caroline,
who makes stories come true

First published in Great Britain in 2000 by
Frances Lincoln Limited, 4 Torriano Mews,
Torriano Avenue, London NW5 2RZ

www.franceslincoln.com

This edition published in 2008

British Library Cataloguing in Publication Data available on request

ISBN 978-1-84507-086-1

Printed and bound by CPI Group (UK) Ltd, Croydon CR0 4YY

3 5 7 9 8 6 4

Starring Grace

MARY HOFFMAN

Illustrations by Caroline Binch

F

FRANCES LINCOLN
CHILDREN'S BOOKS

Contents

Grace is a girl who loves stories. Of course she also loves her Ma, her Nana and Paw-Paw the cat, who are the family she lives with. And her Papa, who lives in the Gambia, West Africa, with his second wife Jatou and their children Neneh and Bakary. You can read about them all in Amazing Grace *and* Grace and Family. *But this book is about how Grace loves stories.*

She is always acting out the stories she knows with her friends. And if there isn't a story that is quite right, she just makes one up...

Grace and the Big Top

It was the beginning of the holidays, and the weeks stretched out ahead of Grace like a new country to explore. Her family weren't going away on a holiday, but later Ma was getting some time off and Nana was going to visit a friend.

Grace didn't mind. Some of her friends were going away to camp, but four were going to be around all summer: her best friend Aimee, plus Kester and Raj and Maria.

"Ma," asked Grace, right at the beginning of summer, "can we have our headquarters here in our flat?"

"Who's 'we'?" asked Ma.

"Me and Aimee and the others. We are the only ones not going away anywhere and I'm the only one with no brothers and sisters to get in the way. Besides, we've got a garden. So can we play here every day? They could bring packed lunch, just like at school."

"That's OK with me, as long as you don't eat me right out of cookies," said Ma. "But you must check with Nana. She's the one who will be home all day with you."

Nana didn't mind. "I like having lots of kids around. You know that, Grace."

It was true. All the children in the neighbourhood seemed to treat Grace's nana as if she were their own grandmother, and that was mainly because she treated them all as if they were her own grandchildren.

So every day Grace's four friends gathered at her flat and thought of things they could be. In the first week they were pirates, then mountaineers, then knights, then aliens. By Friday, they had run out of new things to play.

"We should be a gang and give ourselves a name," said Kester.

"What?" said Aimee. "Like the Famous Five?"

"But we're not famous," objected Grace. "We'd have to be the Five No One Has Heard Of."

"That doesn't sound very exciting," said Raj. "How about the Red Hand Gang?"

"But we don't do crimes," said Maria.

"What *do* we do?" asked Aimee. "We just muck about and have fun."

"We have adventures," said Grace. "That's what we do. And we need a new one." Just then Nana came out and showed them a brightly-coloured advertisement that had been put through the letterbox. It said:

THE CIRCUS IS COMING!

SIGNOR SPARKY'S ONE-DAY SPECTACLE!

See the Flying Fandango Sisters, Horatio the Fire-Eater, Manuel the Magnificent, the Strongest Man in the World, Lady Magnolia and her Famous Troupe of Dancing Horses, the Breathtaking Balancing Act of Boris the Brave Tightrope Walker, the Incredible Antics of the Gravity-Defying Garibaldi Family of Acrobats, and our Own Beloved Clowns, Bongo and Bertie. All hosted by your Ringmaster, the Supreme, the Incomparable SIGNOR SPARKY!

Well, after that there was no question about what the children would be playing for the rest of the day. Grace got Nana to promise she would take her to the circus on Saturday, then the gang set to work in the backyard.

First they made a big circle with string and pegs. Then Grace rummaged in her dressing-up box. She found lots of flowery dresses and bright scarves that had been Nana's and, best of all, a collapsible black hat.

"That's what you call an opera hat," said Nana, shaking the flat black circle so that it turned into a top hat. "It belonged to your grandpa."

"Can we have it for a ringmaster's hat?" said Grace.

"Why not?" said Nana. "There's a cane too. Your grandpa used to tap-dance."

"It should be a whip, really," said Grace. "But we don't have any animals, and besides, a whip is cruel, so a cane is better. It could be a magic wand too."

So now they had a ring and a ringmaster's outfit. Nana put her foot down about tightrope-walking along the clothes-line, trapeze acts hanging from the tree swing or any form of fire-eating. But that still left lots of acts.

Being acrobats was the most popular one. Everybody wanted to be a Garibaldi and there was lots of rolling around, doing somersaults and leapfrogging.

When they were tired of that, Kester said he was going to be Manuel the Magnificent and do some strong things. First he picked up a deck-chair with one hand – almost. Then he got the others to tie him up in a skipping rope and burst out of it. Actually, he sort of untied it, but it looked good.

"I know," said Grace and she got out her face paints and gave Kester a curly black moustache. "Now you really look the part."

"I want to be Lady Magnolia," said Maria, "but we'll have to make up the horses."

Grace dressed Maria in bright scarves and gave her an old-hobby horse to ride. Raj and Aimee wanted to be Bongo and Bertie the clowns. Some more face paint soon gave them red noses and big smiles.

"You'll have to be Signor Sparky, Grace," said Aimee.

Grace didn't mind at all wearing Grandpa's top hat and waving the cane. When they had all done a lot more practising, it was time for Ma to come home from work. Grace was ready for her.

"Roll up, roll up!" she shouted, as soon as Ma was inside the door. "Come to the circus!... Nana too," she added in her ordinary voice.

So Ma and Nana sat in deckchairs drinking iced tea, while Grace introduced all the acts. Kester escaped from the skipping-rope, Maria galloped round the ring on her hobby-horse and even jumped through Grace's old hula hoop. Raj and Maria sprayed each other with silly string and made lots of mess with buckets of water. Then everyone changed back into shorts and T-shirts and became Garibaldis, but they got very wet because of all the water the clowns had spilt on the grass.

At the end, Grace quickly put her top hat back on so she could introduce all the circus performers to take their bows.

"Bravo! Hooray!" shouted Ma and Nana, clapping as hard as they could.

After tea the circus acts all went home, but Grace kept the top hat on for supper and even wore it in the bath.

"Nana says we can go to the circus tomorrow. We can, can't we Ma?" she said at bedtime.

"I dare say we can," said Ma. "But I doubt

they'll be a patch on your circus."

"But they'll have real horses and all the things Nana wouldn't let us do, like fire-eating."

"Nana was quite right about that," said Ma.

The next day, Grace could hardly contain her excitement. She fidgeted all morning and ate her lunch so fast that she couldn't remember what it was.

In the afternoon they went to the local park, where a big striped tent was now standing. They took Aimee with them, and Grace insisted on wearing the top hat. All the children in the neighbourhood seemed to have read Signor Sparky's advertisement and persuaded their parents to bring them to the circus. Kester and Raj and Maria were in the ticket queue and they all got seats quite close together.

There was a real band playing "Rum-tum-tiddle-iddle-um-tum-tara" circus music. Then there was a big drum roll and Signor Sparky strode into the centre of the ring. He had a red suit and a black top hat, a long black whip and a megaphone, through which he shouted "Roll up! Roll Up!" in the most satisfactory way.

The next hour and a half was total magic. The

children laughed at the clowns, gasped at the tight-rope walker and loved the Garibaldis. Lady Magnolia wore a sparkly pink leotard and had huge pink plumes in her hair and on her bottom, and she rode two grey horses at the same time. Manuel the Magnificent ended his act by lifting Lady Magnolia right off the ground. And he *did* have a curly black moustache which looked perfectly real.

After the interval, Signor Sparky asked for a volunteer from the audience and every child in the tent waved their arms in the air. Then his eye lighted on Grace. He picked up his megaphone and said in a loud voice, "I'll have the little girl with the top hat. I could do with an assistant ringmaster."

So Grace got to join the circus. She was given the megaphone and told to announce Horatio the fire-eater. She was so close to him, she could feel the heat of the flaming torches. Then there was a knife-throwing act, jugglers and more from the clowns. Bongo squirted water from a flower in his buttonhole right into Grace's eye!

"And FINALLY," shouted Signor Sparky, "before I introduce our last act, let's give a big hand to our little ringmaster, Signorina Gracia!"

There was lots of clapping and Grace went back to her seat.

"Lucky!" whispered Aimee.

The last act was the Flying Fandango Sisters on the trapeze, and after that the circus was over.

"Did you have a good day?" asked Ma, as she tucked Grace into bed.

"The best!" said Grace. "I've been in the real circus."

"Yes," said Ma. "Two circuses in two days. But I think you'll sleep more comfortably if you take that hat off!"

Grace and the Haunted House

The week after the circus felt a bit flat. After a few half-hearted attempts to learn juggling – which was much harder than it looked in the big top – the children tired of their circus acts and were ready for a new adventure.

"We could be ghostbusters," suggested Kester.

"But there are no ghosts to bust," objected Maria.

"There's no such thing as ghosts anyway," said Raj scornfully.

"What about the haunted house, Grace?" asked Aimee.

Everybody sat up and looked expectantly at Grace. "Well," she began slowly, "we don't know that it *is* haunted for sure."

"We always used to call it that, though," said Aimee.

It was true. The year before, Grace and Aimee had become obsessed with the house whose back garden backed on to Grace's. For weeks they had played a game that the house was haunted, but Ma had got cross and told them not to be silly. Like Raj, Ma didn't believe in ghosts and she thought it was a bad game to play.

That's why Grace was hesitant about telling the others about it now. But they needed a new game and the haunted house was temptingly close by. Besides, everyone had comics with ghosts in them, and they all read books and saw films that were spooky. In fact, it was the most popular sort of entertainment among their schoolfriends.

"Go on, Grace," said Kester. "Tell us about the house."

"It's *that* one," said Grace, settling into her story-telling position with her back against the tree, and pointing to the house beyond the fence. Four pairs of eyes obediently swivelled round to look.

"Ever since we've lived here," went on Grace, "which is as long as I can remember, we've never seen anyone in that garden. It's all overgrown, with long weeds and nettles, and the house has bars on all the windows."

"Perhaps it's empty," suggested Raj.

"No," said Grace. "The postman and the paperboy both call there, and once a week groceries come in a van."

"Maybe it's a hideout for thieves," suggested Maria.

"Or a safe house for witness protection," said Kester.

"Could be," said Grace, "but that doesn't explain the howling in the night."

This produced the desired effect, since her four friends asked with one voice, "What howling in the night?"

"You remember, Aimee," said Grace. "I told you about it last year. It doesn't happen every night. But sometimes it wakes me up. An eerie, ghosty sort of noise that floats through the darkness."

"What does it sound like?" asked Maria.

"Like a soul in torment," said Grace, and gave them a bloodcurdling demonstration.

"I vote we go over the fence and explore," said Raj, jumping to his feet.

Now there was going to be trouble, thought Grace. She knew that Nana wouldn't approve of their going into the neighbouring garden, but she also knew that Nana was having a little nap. And besides, all the others had voted in favour. She couldn't hold out against them, particularly when she was the one who had told them about the house.

So over the fence they went. The garden was waist-high with grass that had not been cut for years. Where the flower beds used to be, there was nothing but nettles, and there were brambles hidden in the long grass. The ghosthunters got a lot of scratches on their legs and arms as they cautiously approached the house.

It wasn't full of towers and pointed roofs like a haunted house in the movies. It was a small, square house, with small, square windows.

"Look," hissed Aimee. "There are the bars."

It was true. Every window had a set of bars like the kind you see on the windows of jewellers' shops.

"Maybe an eccentric millionaire lives there," whispered Maria.

"Yeah," agreed Kester. "There's probably loads of jewels and gold stuff lying around and the millionaire is scared of burglars."

"What do you think, Grace?" asked Aimee.

"I think we should go back," said Grace. She was trying to remember something Nana had told her about the house.

"Don't be wet," said Kester. "We've only just got here."

Just then, an eerie shriek pierced the still air of the overgrown garden. The children stood frozen with terror, then raced for the fence, tearing their clothes on thorns as they ran. They tumbled back into Grace's yard, trembling.

"Now do you believe me?" said Grace, although she herself hadn't really believed that the house was haunted until she heard the howling in broad daylight.

"It's haunted, all right," said Aimee, her eyes as big as saucers.

"There must be some explanation," said Raj.

"But what?" asked Kester.

"And what do we do about it?" asked Maria.

But no one had any ideas. Nana was most suspicious when she called them in to wash their hands before lunch. "What on earth do you find to do in our pocket handkerchief of a back garden to get you all so filthy? And how did you get those scratches?"

Grace made up a story about teasing Paw-Paw the cat and the children kept their worst wounds out of sight while Grace fetched the antiseptic cream.

The children ate their sandwiches and crisps while they discussed a plan.

"We need proper ghost-hunting equipment," said Kester. "We could make some out of odds and ends."

"Yes, but it wouldn't have real electricity or plasma in it," said Raj, "so it wouldn't really work. It would only be pretend."

"But you think ghosts are pretend, anyway," said Maria, and Raj had no answer to that.

So they went to Grace's recycling bins and found cardboard tubes and boxes that looked quite good when stuck together and coloured with felt-tip pen. But there was only enough for one ghost-hunting pack. They drew straws to see who should carry it, and Kester won. The others would have to be decoys and reporters.

"One of us should go round to the front and ring the doorbell," said Maria.

"I'll do it," said Raj. "And I'll keep whoever

opens the door chatting, while you try and get in the back."

"No one will open the door," said Grace. "Whoever lives in that house really doesn't like people."

"Well, it's our best chance," said Maria. "Let's try."

The ghost-hunters climbed over the fence again and through the long grass. There was one nasty moment, when they heard the grass rustling behind them, but it turned out to be Paw-Paw stalking them as part of a game of his own.

The back of the house was just as still and blank as before. The window-frames were all painted brown and you couldn't see through the metal grids, because there were beige-coloured curtains on the inside and they were all tightly drawn. Raj slipped round to the front of the house and the others tried the back door. Grace felt really bad about it – it felt too much like burgling. But the door was firmly locked anyway.

"It'll be no good if someone *does* answer the front door," groaned Kester. "We can't get in the back."

They all heard the doorbell ring at the same time. Raj rang three times, very loudly. The others heard a movement inside the house. The doorbell rang again. Then someone crept up behind the children. They jumped several feet in the air. It was Raj.

"What are you doing here?" said Aimee, "You nearly gave us a heart attack."

Raj was panting. "I rang the bell, but no one came. Then this van drew up and a man came out and walked up to the front door. He gave me a suspicious look, so I bolted."

"He's probably a conspirator," said Maria excitedly.

"No, wait," said Grace. "It's Monday afternoon, isn't it? That's when the grocery van comes."

Just then a voice came calling over the gardens. "Gra-a-ace! GRACE! Where are you?"

"Oh no," groaned Grace. "It's Nana. She'll know we've been in this garden. We are going to be in *so* much trouble."

"And just why are you in my garden?" said a voice from the haunted house. One of the curtains was drawn back, a window had been opened and an ancient face covered in wrinkles was peering out through the bars.

"Stay where you are," said the face and the children heard the unlocking of the back door. There was enough clanking of chains to satisfy the keenest ghost-hunter. The children stood stock-still, caught between the wrath of Nana and whatever was going to come out of the back door of the haunted house.

It was a tiny old lady, the sort you see in fairy tale illustrations. She walked very slowly with a stick, and her hands were gnarled and twisted, "like a witch", thought Grace – but her face was kind and her dark eyes were bright in her wrinkled face. She turned to Raj. "Why were you ringing my doorbell, young man? I saw you from the front window, while I was waiting for my groceries." Her voice was deep and she had a foreign accent.

Raj didn't know what to say. The old woman looked at Kester, with his bundle of tubes and boxes. "What's that contraption?" she asked.

"It's for catching ghosts," said Kester, who was a truthful boy.

There was a funny, rusty, grating noise and the children realised that the old woman was trying to laugh.

"Did you think I was a ghost, then?" she asked.

"Not exactly," said Grace, "but we heard these ghostly noises coming from your house. We're really very sorry. We didn't mean to disturb you."

Just then, Paw-Paw came stalking out from the grass and rubbed himself round the old woman's legs. Grace held her breath.

"Oh, what a beautiful pusskin," said the old woman, and bent to stroke him.

"He's our cat," said Grace. "We call him Paw -Paw."

"Good name for a cat," said the old woman. "I call mine Jauler, which is German for 'Howler'. I wonder if you can guess why?"

A long, pointed, handsome face peeped round the door, at the level of the woman's ankles. It was chocolate-coloured with blue eyes. It was followed by a cream-coloured thin body with very long legs. When he saw Paw-Paw, he arched his back and hissed. Then he let out a long unearthly howl. At first the children froze, then they relaxed and began to smile.

"Here is your ghost, no?" said the old woman.

Grace breathed a sigh of relief. Not only was the house not haunted, but the old woman didn't seem cross with them for trespassing in her garden. Then she remembered Nana.

"We'd better go," she said politely. "And we really are sorry that we thought your house was haunted. It was only a game."

"Ah," said the old woman sadly. "I didn't say it wasn't haunted. Only that my cat is no ghost. But, listen, your grandmother is calling you. You can tell her I asked you to help find my cat. She knows I don't like him to go out."

Grace gasped. "You know my nana?"

"A little," said the old woman. "I don't have many friends."

"We'll be your friends, if you like," said Aimee.

The old woman looked at her and a series of strange expressions flitted across her face.

"I should like that," she said. "Come back tomorrow and I'll have some cakes ready for you." Then she picked up her Siamese cat, who draped himself over her shoulders like a scarf, and went back indoors. The children heard the bolts and chains.

"Cakes!" said Kester, as they ran back through the long grass. "That's just like the witch in the gingerbread house. She probably wants to eat us."

"Don't be so silly," said Maria. "She was a nice old lady."

"Nana won't let us go back unless she knows it's safe," said Grace. "She doesn't let me talk to strangers."

But Nana took a lot of calming down, once the children had scrambled back over the fence. After a while she listened properly to what they were telling her.

"That's Gerda Myerson," she said eventually. "I'm amazed she asked you to help her. Gerda keeps herself to herself."

"But why?" asked Grace, who didn't feel the whole mystery of the house had been explained. After all, the old woman herself had agreed it was haunted. "And why does she have all those locks and bars?"

Nana hesitated. "Gerda Myerson had some very bad experiences during the war," she said at last. "Very bad. All her family was killed and she was imprisoned for a very long time. She survived and came to live in this country. But she finds it hard to trust people and she keeps her house all locked up, to make herself feel safe."

"Can we go and see her again tomorrow?"

asked Grace. "She invited us and said she'd give us cake."

Nana laughed. "Well, I see she knows the best way to get you to be her friends. Yes, you can go. It's a good sign that Gerda asked you. Perhaps she finds children less frightening than grown-ups. But promise me you will never, ever go out of this garden again without telling me where you are going. You scared me out of my wits."

And the ghost-hunters all promised.

Grace Goes on Safari

Next day, the gang were all for going straight back into the overgrown garden.

"Not yet," said Aimee. "She won't have had time to make the cakes."

"You don't know that she's going to make them," said Raj. "She might have had some delivered by the grocer."

"Why would an old lady living on her own order enough cakes to feed five children?" asked Kester.

"I would, if I was an old lady," said Maria.

Grace said, "Let's think what we're going to do when we get there. I've had an idea."

Everyone looked at Grace.

"It's the perfect kind of garden to be a jungle," she said.

Everyone started to talk at once. They hadn't played explorers yet this summer and Grace was right: the haunted house's garden was the perfect place.

"We'll need supplies," said Grace. "And sun hats. And some things to be wild animals."

As usual, Nana was roped in to help with what they needed for their game. She didn't seem to mind their going back into the next door garden.

"You'll need lots of bottles of water if you're going on safari," she said. "The jungle is a thirsty place."

They found all sorts of old hats to wear as sola topis. Nana let Grace have hers, the one she had worn when they went to The Gambia. It really did look a bit like a safari hat. And the star of the animal collection, which was mainly soft bears and rabbits, was a huge wooden crocodile with white teeth, which they had brought back from West Africa.

"We should have a tent," said Raj. "Have you got one, Grace?"

Grace hadn't, but instead they took some old sheets and a clothes-drying rack.

"We'll have to cut some grass before we can pitch a tent," said Maria. "We need a machete."

Nana didn't have a machete, but she gave them a rather blunt pair of garden shears, with

lots of warnings to be careful.

It was a good job that old Mrs Myerson knew they were coming. When she looked out of her back window, she saw five hats advancing through the grass and strange objects held high, including a large crocodile.

The children knocked on the back door.

"Good morning," said Grace, when the old woman opened the door. "I hope we're not too early. We wondered if we could play safaris in your garden."

"I see you're all dressed for the part," said Mrs Myerson. "You play as much as you like, and when you've had enough, knock again and I'll have a treat ready for you."

It was a glorious morning. The sun shone and it was very hot, just like in the real jungle. The children pretended that the flies were mosquitoes. They pulled leaves off one of the bigger weeds and used them to wave in front of their faces. Paw-Paw joined them and became a real tiger in the long grass.

They found a very small stagnant pond in one corner of the garden, which Grace said was the great grey-green greasy Limpopo river. It was full of frogs and looked very realistic when they put Grace's crocodile on the bank.

Mrs Myerson's garden was no bigger than Grace's, but it seemed huge because it was so wild and overgrown. They pretended all the brambles in the grass were snakes, and they had to avoid being bitten.

When they got tired, they took turns cutting a patch of grass near the house with the shears, and set up their clothes-horse tent in the clearing they had made. There was room for two in it if they squeezed in very tightly. The others threw themselves down on the grass.

"I'm famished," said Kester. "Let's see about those cakes."

Mrs Myerson hobbled out with a tray of delicious-smelling cakes, which were a funny shape, twisted like pretzels, but covered with white icing sugar. They were full of sultanas and almonds and the taste of cinnamon.

She sat on an old kitchen chair outside her back door and watched the children eat like real hungry explorers.

"It is nice to sit in the sun again," she said in her deep rusty voice, "and I see you have been cutting my grass."

"I hope you don't mind," said Grace. "We needed somewhere for the tent."

But immediately Grace felt sorry that they had only cut the grass to fit their game.

As soon as Mrs Myerson had gone indoors, an idea began to form in her mind for another game just as good.

"*The Secret Garden*," she said. "That's what this is. We could make it all nice for her again and then she could sit out in it."

"That's a girl's story," said Raj. "And if we cut all the grass we won't be able to play safari any more."

"But we've played that already," said Grace, who was always looking for new games. "Besides, there are boys in *The Secret Garden*. There's Dickon, who is brilliant with animals and Colin, who is..."

"Wet," said Kester. "I'm not being him."

"But he stops being wet when he meets Mary," said Maria. "I should be her because I've got the right sort of name."

"I don't mean we should act out *The Secret Garden*," said Grace. "There are only three children in it and five of us. I mean we could make up a secret garden type of story of our own, while we clear this one up for Mrs Myerson. After all, she did make us lovely cakes – and she didn't tell on us to Nana yesterday."

In the end they all agreed. But they had to go back to Grace's and explain their plan to Nana. She thought it was a good idea and gave them some gardening gloves and trowels and some black bags for the weeds and boxes for the brambles.

As soon as they had had their lunch, the safari team went back into the wild garden.

"We're still explorers," said Grace. "Only we've stumbled on a secret garden in the heart of the jungle. We need to make a big clearing, so that ..."

"So that we can reach the holy temple in the middle of the garden," said Aimee.

"Yes," said Kester. "And in the temple there's an old statue with a precious ruby in it."

"Worth millions of pounds," said Raj. "And if we find it, we can keep it."

It was only a small garden and there were five of them, so it shouldn't have taken long to tidy up. But Nana hadn't given them any very sharp tools and there had been no weeding done for years. Cutting the grass was very hard, too, as it was damp. When they had cleared a patch, it looked stubbly and yellow instead of smooth and green.

"Hey, I've found a wild orchid!" called Maria, who was weeding in a flower-bed.

They all came to see the bright red flower she had cleared from under the weeds. It was some sort of lily, but it looked exotic enough to be an orchid in the weedy flower-bed.

"That'll cheer the old lady up," said Kester.

They speeded up after finding the flower, and by the end of the afternoon the side passage was full of bags and boxes of grass-cuttings and weeds. The old jungle had completely disappeared and the late afternoon sun shone on a square of yellow lawn, three dug-over flower-beds and a small pond with reeds and frogs.

The children had found lots of stones and pebbles when they were digging and they piled the best ones up round the pond to look like a rockery. The lumpy ones they put in the boxes with the brambles.

When they had finished, they saw Nana's face smiling over the fence.

"My, you've done a good job!" she said, looking at the secret garden. "Won't Gerda be pleased!"

At that moment, Mrs Myerson came out of her back door. At first she didn't seem pleased at all. She looked at the garden. Her face twisted and there were tears on her cheeks. Then she brushed them away with the back of her hand and smiled.

"Thank you," she said. "Thank you, my little explorers. You have discovered a lovely garden for me. It reminds me of when I was a child, and the world was a sunnier place."

Then she walked across the still-damp grass to speak to Nana.

The explorers ate a huge tea before going home. Their arms and legs ached and they were covered in fresh bramble scratches and nettle stings. But they were all happy.

"It's a pity about the jungle," said Raj.

"And we didn't find a precious jewel," said Kester.

"No" said Maria, "but my orchid was as red as a ruby."

"And the new garden might be as precious as jewels to Mrs Myerson," said Grace.

"I think you all did a very important thing today," said Nana. "Most of your games are just for fun and that's just how it should be. But today you played a game that helped a frightened person come out and walk in the sunshine of her own garden."

Grace had been feeling bad for a whole day about lying to Nana. Now she just had to own up.

"Yesterday we thought Mrs Myerson was a ghost," she said. "We went into her garden to find out. She didn't really ask us to help her catch her cat."

Nana looked serious for a moment. "She is a bit like a ghost. Or she used to be. You kids seem to be bringing her back to life."

"I thought she was a witch when we first saw her," admitted Aimee.

"Well, honey," said Nana, "There's more to people than what they look like."

"Yeah," said Kester. "She makes great cakes."

They all laughed.

"That's two things you explorers discovered today, then," said Nana.

Grace Blasts Off

Grace was having a hard time. Nana wasn't there. She had gone on holiday all by herself – a thing Grace couldn't remember ever happening before in her whole life.

"Of course you must go," Ma had said, when Nana got the invitation from her old friend Coralita in Texas. "It will be the holiday of a lifetime."

So Nana had gone – for two whole weeks – and Grace wished she had gone with her. It wasn't that she and Ma didn't love each other, because of course they did, very much. But they weren't used to being on their own together. As long as Grace could remember, Nana had always been there, ready to hear about what had happened at school, or happy to tell Grace one of her stories, or just singing in the kitchen while she cooked the dinner.

Now Grace was being looked after during the

day by Aimee's mum and the gang had to play at Aimee's house. Aimee's mum brought Grace back each evening when Ma got in from work.

And when Ma did get in, Grace was usually bursting to tell what had happened during her day, how Aimee had new trainers just like the kind Grace wanted, or what games the gang had played. But Ma was always so tired when she got home. She sat on the sofa and kicked off her leather shoes and said, "Make me a cup of tea, will you, honey?" and "Could you fetch my slippers, please, sweetie? I've had such a day of it."

Of course Grace didn't mind doing these things, but she wanted Ma to listen to stuff about her day too. And Ma *would* listen, sort of. But she kept yawning and often, after she had drunk her tea, she would nod off for a bit and Grace just had to be patient, watch TV and wait for her to wake up.

And Ma didn't seem to know any stories like Nana's, except what had happened at the hospital – how there were never enough beds for the sick people who needed them, and how she was rushed off her feet trying to find somewhere to put everyone.

When she woke up again, it was Ma who made the dinner, and she didn't sing while she did it. Grace helped her and that was their best time together. Grace made cold drinks for them both and laid the table and she and Ma did chat then. But, although Grace felt mean even thinking it, Ma didn't make such nice food as Nana did.

Grace missed Nana's fried chicken and black-eyed beans. Ma would just pick up something ready-made from the supermarket on the way home from work, which could be cooked quickly in the oven or microwave. Grace didn't say anything, because she knew how hard Ma worked and how tired she got. But she was a bit tired of frozen pizza and oven chips.

The second week, when Grace came home, she found a letter on the mat with a beautiful stamp on it. It had blue flowers and a Texas postmark.

Nana! thought Grace. But the letter was addressed to Ma.

As soon as Ma opened the door, Grace met her with a cup of tea and her slippers.

"Sit down, sit down, Ma," she said excitedly. "Here's your tea. And here's a letter from Nana!

Open it and read it to me, please!"

"All right, all right," said Ma. "Let me get my breath." But she did open the letter. "Look, here's one inside just for you," she said. "And a photo. Oh, my! What *has* Nana done?"

Grace took the photo. And there was Nana's lovely familiar face but she was dressed as an astronaut! Grace's eyes got bigger and bigger. "Nana hasn't gone up in space, has she?" she asked.

Ma laughed until the tears ran down her cheeks.

"Oh, Grace, you should see your face! I don't think so, but let's read our letters and find out."

Grace's letter was hard to read. She had never seen Nana's handwriting before. But what it said was very exciting. Nana had been to the NASA Space Center and seen Mission Control and eaten special space ice-cream. And then she had had her photo taken in a studio that made her look like an astronaut.

"Well, doesn't that beat everything!" said Ma. "My mother, the astronaut. I know that some older people are going up in space now, but I never thought I'd see your nana dressed up in a

space suit and helmet."

Grace's eyes were shining. She had never thought of being an astronaut, but now her imagination was working overtime.

"Do you know any stories about space, Ma?" she asked.

"Well, I can tell you about the night I stayed up to watch the first people walk on the moon," said Ma. "In fact, why don't we go out and get a Chinese meal tonight and I'll tell you over dinner? I'm getting sick of my own cooking."

It was the best night since Nana had been away on holiday. They had chow mein and fried rice and spring rolls and pancakes with a spicy sauce, and Grace ate as much as she possibly could. So did Ma, and she told Grace about when she was a little girl, much younger than Grace was now, and they had seen the first people on the moon.

"We didn't have our own TV then – imagine! – so we went to a neighbour's house. In fact it was Coralita's house, you know, the friend Nana is staying with now. There were about a dozen kids all crammed on the sofa, all very sleepy, because it was way past our bedtime, and then the landing was delayed, so it got even later. I kept dozing off and then your Nana shook me awake and said 'Look, look, Ava, that's the moon and that man coming down the ladder is the first person ever to step on it.' I couldn't believe it. I mean, it was all just like a dusty old desert, not a bit like the shiny, silvery moon Nana used to take me out to see on clear nights."

OK, maybe Ma didn't tell the story as well as Nana would have done, but it was a story all the same and Grace was full of it. At the weekend she borrowed all the space books she could find in the library and played astronauts with the gang. She showed them the photo and told them her Nana was going into space.

"I'm Mae Jemison," said Grace, "and I'm launching my shuttle. Ten ... Nine ... Eight ... Seven ... Six ... Five ... Four ... Three ... Two ... One – BLAST OFF!"

And she ran round the back yard with her arms out wide, flapping them so hard, she nearly did take off. Aimee and Raj and Kester and Maria were all round at Grace's house and there was only one game they wanted to play. They pretended there was no gravity by walking slowly round the yard, taking huge steps and bouncing slowly up and down.

"I'm going to be an astronaut when I grow up," said Grace.

"So am I," said Kester. "It's the best job. You get to be weightless and eat dried food so you don't have to wash up."

"Me too," said the others.

"But we can't be astronauts without a spaceship," said Grace. "Let's build one!"

So they found a lot of cardboard boxes and some crates that Nana's marmalade oranges had come in and tied them together with string. It didn't look very like a spaceship when they had finished, but two small astronauts could just about squeeze into the "capsule" at the same time. They took turns.

But blasting off was difficult; the spaceship just toppled over.

"I know," said Grace. "Let's prop it up against the tree, so it's upright."

It was Grace's turn to be captain. Aimee was her navigator and the others were Mission Control. It was much more difficult to get into the spaceship now it was propped against the tree.

"OK," said Raj. "All systems are go. Prepare for lift-off. TEN ... NINE ... EIGHT ..."

But by the time he got to THREE, the spaceship was wobbling alarmingly. Aimee was trying to make herself more comfortable in the crate and Grace was trying to keep it steady. On the count of ONE – BLAST-OFF! the whole contraption collapsed and Grace and Aimee fell out in a heap.

"Ow!" yelled Aimee. "You're sitting on my hand! It really hurts."

Grace had a bump on her head that was growing before their eyes. But Aimee was clutching her wrist with her other hand and her face had gone very white. Hearing the noise, Ma came running out into the yard. She took one look at the astronauts and sent Mission Control home. Then she took the two girls to the doctor.

Grace was given a big plaster on her forehead and Aimee had her arm put in a sling.

"It's all right," said the doctor to Ma. "It's not broken. Just a sprain. And Grace is going to be fine."

"Whatever were you doing?" said Ma, on the way home.

"We were launching into space," said Grace. "Only our spaceship fell over."

"It was brilliant," said Aimee, happily. Her wrist was throbbing but she didn't mind.

"Well, now," said Ma. "It's a well-known fact that space travel is dangerous. So I'm going to say right now – and I think Aimee's mum will agree with me – that there are to be no more astronaut games."

"That's OK," said Grace. "We don't want to play astronauts any more. I want to be a doctor now!"

Calling Doctor Grace

As soon as Nana got back from Texas, she heard all about the astronaut adventure. Then Grace said, "Nana, you're not looking at all well. I think you should see the doctor."

"I'm fine, Grace," said Nana, "just a bit tired from the flight."

"I don't think she means just any old doctor," said Ma.

"Oh, I see," said Nana. "You mean Doctor Grace? I'm always glad to see her."

Playing doctors had always been one of Grace's favourite games. Last birthday, Ma had given her a dressing-up outfit with a white coat and a wonderful doctor's bag full of instruments and bandages. (Ma secretly hoped that Grace might really be a doctor when she grew up.)

So Nana had to lie down on the sofa and have her temperature taken. "Hmm," said Grace, holding Nana's wrist. "A bad case of anti-rhino. You must take these pills."

"Fine," said Nana. "Would it be all right to take them with a cup of tea?"

"Yes," said Grace, "but only after I've bandaged your leg."

"I didn't know anti-rhino affected the legs," said Ma. "I'd better put the kettle on."

"Oh yes," said Grace. "It does when it's a bad case. It starts in the head, but it goes to the legs if you don't get the pills in time."

Soon Nana had a fine bandage on her leg. And since she really *was* feeling quite tired, she didn't mind sitting still and taking her medicine.

"How about you?" Grace asked Ma. "I could check up on your heart."

"You checked it only yesterday," said Ma. "But you can do it again, as long as I can sit down and talk to Nana about her holiday."

Grace didn't mind. She was the kind of doctor who only needed her patients to keep still. So she listened to Ma's heart with her stethoscope and tested her blood pressure and wrote up her notes on the case.

Patient's name: Ma
Illness: Heart sounds broken
Treatment: Bandages

Grace took another of her long bandages and started to wind it round Ma's chest.

"What's this?" said Ma, reading her notes. "My heart's not broken."

"Patients aren't allowed to know what's wrong with them," said Grace. "It spoils the treatment."

"But surely I should know whether my heart's broken or not," Ma protested. "I mean, it wouldn't work, would it?"

"It'll work if you let me bandage it," said Grace firmly, but she noticed that Ma and Nina exchanged funny looks when they thought she couldn't see.

Grace soon ran out of bandages, so she went off to see if Paw-Paw needed an injection. She was the kind of doctor who didn't mind treating animals.

The game got even better when her friends came round, because Aimee still had her arm in a real sling. Grace set up a hospital in the back yard, putting her patients on deck chairs. To make things look more realistic, Grace got her face paints and Kester painted big red cuts and purple bruises on to Raj and Maria. Ma had quite a shock when she came out with lemonade and biscuits.

"Gracious! That looks bad, Raj. How did it happen?" she asked.

"I was bitten by a tiger," said Raj proudly.

"And I fell off a mountain," said Maria.

"You're lucky you only got a bruise," said Ma. "You might have broken something."

"She did," said Grace. "She broke everything. It's a good job you brought those bandages back. And I'll need some splints too."

By the end of the day, everyone had a sling or a bandage or a splint. Even Grace, who let Maria borrow her doctor's outfit, had a big bandage on her foot and was walking with a stick. Of course they all had to take them off before they went home and Ma insisted that they wash off the face paint, in case their mums were frightened.

Grace rolled up her bandages and re-packed her bag while Ma and Nana made the supper. Then she noticed that Ma looked different. She was wearing a new dress and had put on some lipstick.

"Are you going out, Ma?" she asked.

"Yes, honey. I'm going to see a film with a friend. Nana will be here to look after you."

"That will be nice, won't it Grace?" said Nana. "We can have a nice long talk. And your poor ma hasn't been out for all the time I've been away."

"Yes, she has," said Grace. "She went to a Chinese restaurant with me. And she went to work every day."

Somehow, Grace felt a bit grumpy about Ma going out on Nana's first night back. And she felt even grumpier when the doorbell rang and she saw that Ma's friend was a man.

"Grace," said Ma. "I want you to meet my friend Vincent. Vince, this is Grace. And you know my mother."

"How do you do?" said Vincent. "Good to meet you Grace. I see you take after your ma."

Grace let him shake her hand, but already she didn't like him.

When they had gone, Nana said, "Why don't you give me a complete check-up, Grace? That anti-rhino seems to be coming back."

Grace gave Nana a very thorough check-up and lots of medicine. It was only coloured water and Nana was very good about taking it. In fact, she was a very good patient altogether, but Grace wasn't happy. She couldn't forget the way Vincent had put his hand under Ma's elbow as they went out of the door.

"What's the matter, Grace?" asked Nana. "Am I a hopeless case?"

"No," said Grace. "But I don't want Ma to marry Vincent."

"Goodness, child," said Nana. "What put that into your head? She has only known him a short while."

"But he seems to like her," said Grace.

"Yes he does. And that's nice for your ma. She works very hard and she needs a little bit of fun sometimes. It's good for her to have a man friend she can go out with. It doesn't mean they're going to get married."

"Promise?" asked Grace.

"Of course not," said Nana. "Your ma could get married again if she wanted to – she's still young enough."

Grace thought about this. "Is Vincent a doctor?" she asked.

Nana laughed. "No, but he does work at the

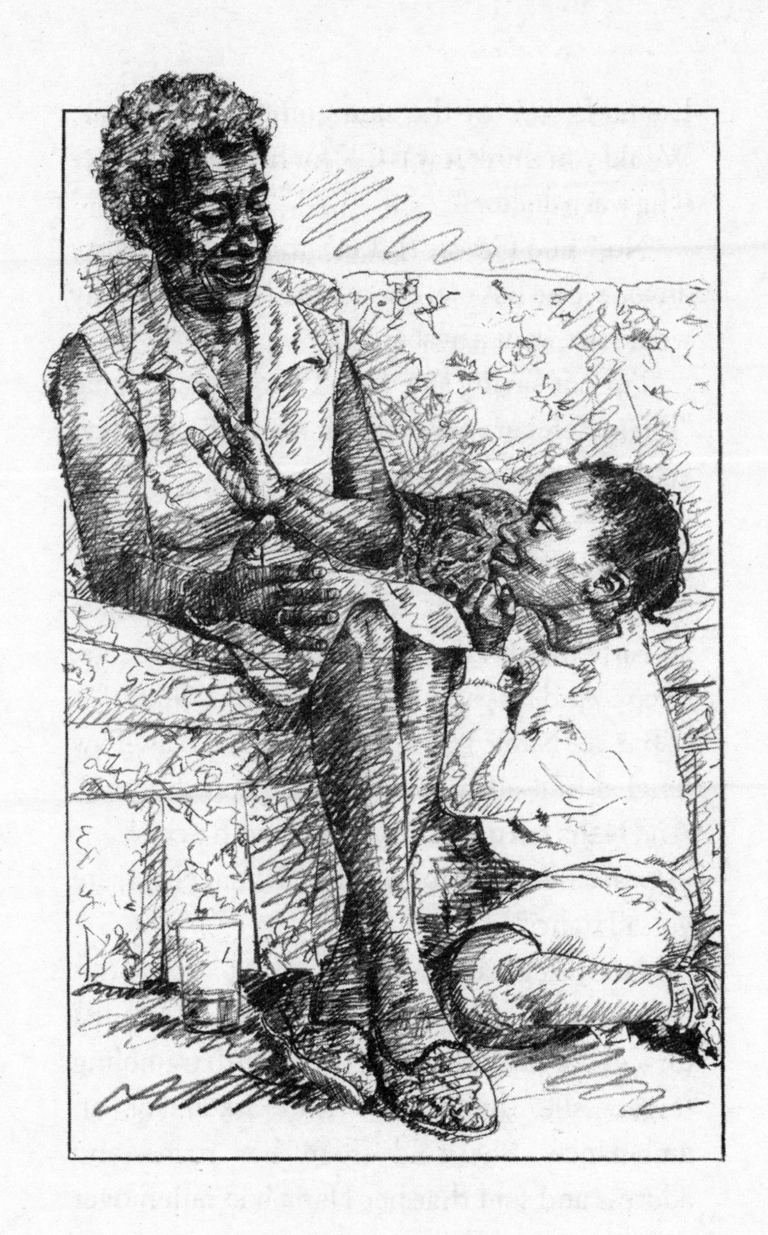

hospital. He's in the same office as your ma. Would you think it was OK for him to marry her if he was a doctor?"

"No," said Grace. "I don't want her to marry anyone. She has me, doesn't she? And you. Why would she want a husband?"

"I'm not saying she does, Grace," said Nana. "But remember your papa got married again, and you didn't like Jatou at first."

This was too big a thought for Grace. It seemed as if her world was turning upside down.

"Well," said Nana. "I think I'm going to have an early night. All that medicine has made me sleepy. And it's past your bedtime, too, Grace."

But as Nana got up off the sofa, Paw-Paw tangled himself in her feet and tripped her up. And Nana fell down on the floor with a crash.

Grace flew over to her side. "Nana, Nana, are you all right?"

Nana just groaned.

"Oh, if only I was really a doctor," wailed Grace. But she knew what to do. With trembling fingers she dialled 999 and asked for an ambulance. She told them her name and address and said that her Nana had fallen over and hurt herself.

Then she went back to Nana and put a blanket over her to keep her warm. It seemed like ages, but the ambulance got there quite quickly. It didn't have its siren on, but Grace saw the blue flashing light through the living-room window.

"She's going to be fine," said the paramedic, after checking Nana out. "But we'll have to get her to hospital. Is your mother here?"

"No, she's gone to the pictures," said Grace. "But I don't know which one."

"Then you come along with us and your nana. We'll leave your mother a note, telling her what's happened. And when she comes to the hospital, we'll tell her what a sensible girl you are."

By now, Nana was awake, and she told the paramedics, "Of course Grace knew what to do. She's a doctor. Can't you see her white coat?"

Grace sat beside Nana in the back of the ambulance, and this time the siren screamed through the night as it drove quickly to the hospital.

The doctor let Grace stay while she examined Nana and she had an X-ray. When the film came back, the doctor showed Grace the break in Nana's ankle-bone.

"You see that, doctor?" she said. "That's the end of the tibia."

"Yes, doctor," said Grace. "Will she have to have a bandage?"

"Oh yes," said the hospital doctor. "A big bandage, with plaster on top. And she'll have to walk on crutches for a few weeks."

"Oh, poor Nana!" said Grace.

"But she'll be absolutely fine. She's quite lucky. At her age she might have broken her hip, and that's a lot more serious," said the doctor.

Just then, Ma's face appeared round the cubicle curtains.

"What on earth has happened?" she asked. The doctor explained. "But thanks to your daughter, everything's going to be fine."

Ma gave Grace a hug. "She's a good doctor, isn't she?"

"Yes, she can have a job here any time," said the doctor.

But Grace had a funny feeling that she didn't want to play doctors again for a long time.

Grace the Detective

Nana's accident changed everything. There was no way she could cope with having Grace's friends around every day. In fact, Ma had to rearrange her plans and take her holiday a week early, so that she could look after Nana.

Nana hated all the fuss. "It's only a broken ankle," she said. "I've still got all my wits about me and I can still cook."

But once she was back home, even she had to admit that it was awkward and painful getting about the flat on her crutches. And it was too difficult for her to go shopping or use the vacuum cleaner.

For the first few days she didn't try cooking either – so it was back to pizza and frozen meals. Grace had a lot to do running around fetching things for Nana – like her glasses, or her book, or her knitting, or the phone.

"You're a great nurse as well as a doctor," said Nana.

But Grace wasn't thinking about hospitals any more. There was something else on her mind.

Ever since Nana's fall and Ma taking time off work, they had been seeing more and more of Ma's friend Vincent. He dropped by to take Ma shopping in his car, or he said he was "just passing" and had called in to see how Nana was. He was always taking up space in their sitting room, always sitting in Grace's usual place on the sofa, often a fourth person at dinner, who was served before Grace.

"I hate it," Grace told Aimee, when she went to play at her house.

"Don't you mean *him?*" asked Aimee.

Grace thought about it. "No, I don't think I hate Vincent. He's OK. He's always polite to me and he's really nice to Nana. And I can see he really likes Ma. But we don't need him, and he's always there. He's so *big.*"

Aimee laughed. "Well, he can't help that. My dad's big and I don't mind."

"But he's not my dad!" said Grace sharply. Aimee had reminded her of her worst worry. What if Ma and Vince got married? Then he'd always be there. Would she be expected to call him Dad? Grace already had her own papa, who lived in Africa, and she wasn't about to let anyone take his place.

She told Aimee all this.

"Perhaps you'd better ask your ma," suggested Aimee.

"No," said Grace. "She wouldn't tell me. Besides, he might not have asked her yet. I'll have to find out some other way."

Then she had a brilliant idea.

"I know! I'll spy on them! I'll keep a special notebook and write down all the times he comes round and the things he says, and then I'll ask Ma. I'll have proper evidence then."

"Wouldn't it be better to spy on just him?" said Aimee. "Like a private eye? You might find out he has a wife and ten children."

Grace cheered up. "That would be brilliant!" But then her face fell. "I couldn't do it. I'm not allowed out on my own."

Still, she liked the private eye idea. Detectives was one of her favourite games for playing on her own. Grace went to get her outfit together. She had a battered brown trilby hat of Grandpa's which she pulled down over her eyes and an old raincoat of Ma's which she belted tightly around her middle. She got a notebook and pencil and started watching Ma and Vincent.

MONDAY – Vince to supper
TUESDAY – Vince dropped in for coffee
WEDNESDAY – Vince took Ma shopping
THURSDAY – Vince took Ma to pictures
FRIDAY –

Well, it was Friday today – but Grace could see the pattern already. When Vincent came round that evening to watch a nature programme on TV, he found Grace staring at him and writing notes in her book.

The gang got together as usual on Saturday at Grace's. They had fallen into the pattern of working next door in Mrs Myerson's garden on Saturday mornings. The little lawn was green now and there were lots of brightly-coloured flowers in the beds.

When they had finished, they sprawled on the grass eating home-made gingerbread, while Grace told them about Vincent.

"My mum has a boyfriend," said Maria.

"I didn't say he was my mum's boyfriend,"

said Grace.

"Sounds like it to me," said Kester.

"You can't be sure," said Raj, waving his piece of cake. "Remember how you once said Mrs Myerson would feed us cakes and eat us?"

"Anyway, I don't see what's wrong with it," said Kester. "I wish my mum had a boyfriend. She's been miserable since my dad left."

"But wouldn't you hate having someone taking your dad's place?" asked Grace.

Kester shrugged. "Not really. I'm glad he's not there any more."

Grace's eyes filled with tears. She couldn't imagine feeling the way Kester did. But she blinked them back.

That evening, Vincent was going to take Ma out to dinner. Ma made some pasta and sauce for Nana and Grace before she left. It was quite nice, but after Ma had gone, Nana said to Grace, "Why don't we make some fudge?"

"Are you sure, Nana? Can you manage?"

"Of course! There's not much cooking in fudge, and you can do most of the work."

Soon they were eating crumbly chocolate fudge with hazelnut chunks. They watched a silly comedy on TV and then Grace washed up and helped Nana get ready for bed.

"It's as if I'm babysitting you, instead of the other way round," she said.

"Not so much of the baby," said Nana. "You're granny-sitting, that's all, and a fine job you're doing. Now fetch me my paper, and you'd better be getting ready for bed yourself."

But Grace had other plans. She put on her detective hat and coat and took her notebook, and sat by the living-room window in the dark, watching out for Ma and Vincent. But a private eye who is full of pasta and fudge finds it hard to stay awake, and she soon nodded off.

The sound of a car door slamming woke her up. She heard two people talking and laughing outside the front door. Grace had her nose pressed hard against the window.

SATURDAY – Vince Kissed Ma! she wrote.

But then Ma's key turned in the door and Grace heard her inviting Vincent in for a hot chocolate. "Oh no," thought Grace. "They'll come in here and find me."

She curled herself up small on the window-sill

and hid as quietly as she could behind the curtain. The lights snapped on. In Grace's flat, you got to the kitchen by walking through the living-room. Grace heard the mugs clattering and then the sound of a kettle boiling, while Ma and Vincent talked in low voices.

Then she heard them coming back into the living room. Ma turned on the radio and music began to play softly. The curtain moved, and Grace nearly screamed. It was Paw-Paw, who wanted to see why she was hiding on the window-sill. He was delighted to find Grace behind the curtain, and started purring loudly. Then he tried to climb on her lap, which wasn't really there, because Grace's knees were nearly touching her chest.

But Paw-Paw was a determined cat and he forced his way on to where her lap should have been. One of Grace's legs slipped off the windowsill and Paw-Paw started to "make puddings" on her lap. His claws were sharp and Grace couldn't help herself.

"Ow!" she cried, and fell out from her hiding-place on to the floor with a thud.

Vincent was so startled, he spilled his

chocolate on the sofa. There was a flurry of activity while Ma got a cloth to clean it up, and Vincent kept apologising.

"Don't worry," said Ma grimly. "It wasn't your fault. It's Grace who ought to be saying sorry. What on earth do you think you are playing at, Grace?"

"It's late," said Vincent. "I think I'd better be going."

When he had gone, Ma came and sat Grace down next to her on the sofa.

"Now, what was all that about?" she said. "As if I don't know. Look at you! All dressed up like a detective. You've been spying on me."

Grace hung her head. It was quite true. "I'm sorry, Ma," she said. "I didn't mean to embarrass you. I was just keeping an eye on Vincent."

"Why? What has he done?"

"Well, he has been around here a lot."

"That's not a crime, is it?"

"No."

"Well, detectives are usually on the track of crimes, aren't they? What do you think is wrong with Vince being here?"

"I don't want you to get married!" Grace said.

"Get married! Whatever gave you that idea?"

"I saw him kiss you," said Grace, and she burst into tears.

Ma took Grace into her arms and cuddled her until she stopped crying.

"You see what trouble your games can get you into?" she said. "Vince and I aren't getting married. I've only known him a few months. But we *are* going out together."

"So is he your boyfriend?" asked Grace.

"Yes, I guess you could say he is," said Ma, laughing. "Though that makes us sound like teenagers. Don't you like him?"

"He's OK," said Grace. "I just don't see why you need him when you've got Nana and me."

"Well, why do you need Aimee? And Raj and Maria and Kester? You've got Nana and me, but you still have to have other people in your life, don't you?"

"Ye-es," said Grace. "Are you sure you're not going to marry him?"

"No, honey, I'm not absolutely certain sure. But it's too soon to think about that."

"Do you like him more than Papa?" asked Grace.

Ma sighed. "That's a really hard question. I like him a lot and that's all I'm thinking about at the moment."

Grace snuggled up close to Ma's silky dress. "You smell nice," she said.

"So do you," said Ma. "In fact, you smell of chocolate fudge."

"That's because we made some," said Grace, springing up off the sofa. "And there's lots left in the fridge. Would you like a bit?"

"There's only one thing I'd like more," said Ma, "and that's for you to take off that hat and coat and think of a new game!"

So Grace stopped being a detective and instead dipped pieces of fudge in Ma's chocolate drink. And she went to bed happier than she had been for a long time.

Grace and the Time Machine

Nana was a lot better, so the gang was allowed to come back and play at Grace's place. Ma went back to work and things were more or less back to normal.

But Nana's leg was still in plaster, and even though she could get around very quickly on her crutches, she still found it difficult to bend down or reach up. Grace and the others were always picking things up for her, or climbing up on chairs to get things down from high places.

"It's lovely to have so many extra arms and legs," said Nana gratefully.

"But what about when we're not here?" said Grace. "We should invent something to help you pick up things."

"Yes," said Raj. "Let's be inventors. We can invent all sorts of things."

"Maybe we'll be rich," said Maria.

The next hour was a very messy one in

Grace's kitchen. Every utensil was tipped out of the kitchen drawers and a lot of string and parcel tape was used. Eventually, the inventors proudly presented Nana with a pair of tongs with salad servers and wooden spoons attached to them.

The children made Nana drop her glasses on the rug and then showed her how to pick them up with the tongs, without bending down.

"If that doesn't beat everything!" said Nana. "Thank you. It's a wonderful invention."

But when Ma came home, and the supper was made, they found it difficult to manage without all the bits of the picking-up machine. They had to serve the salad with a spoon and fork, which was OK, and turn the sausages with two more forks, which was awkward, and Nana found it difficult to make gravy without a wooden spoon.

"It was very kind of you to invent this gadget for Nana," said Ma, after they had eaten. "But you know, I think someone has already invented it and I can get it from the hospital."

Next day, Grace's face fell when she saw the grey metal grabber. It was much better than the tong machine.

"So we didn't invent anything after all," she said.

"But you thought of it, Grace," said Ma. "And I didn't. I could have got one of these for Nana weeks ago."

Grace was cheered up a bit. But the others were very disapppointed.

"All that time," said Aimee, "and we just invented something that already existed."

"We just have to think of something that no one else has thought of," said Raj. "That's what real inventors do."

"Oh, is that all?" said Kester. "It should be easy then."

"Don't squabble," said Grace. "We must all think hard of something we wish existed, but doesn't. Something that would be useful to us."

"Grass that doesn't need cutting," said Maria, who was fed up with the blunt shears they had to use on Mrs Myerson's lawn every Saturday.

"Skateboards with brakes," said Kester, who had a big blue bruise on his knee.

"That's what feet are for," said Raj. "I'd like a machine that would read books for you."

How horrible! thought Grace, but she didn't

say anything, because she knew Raj found reading very hard.

"I think," said Aimee, "I'd like something that would make you taller, but not hurt."

Aimee was very self-conscious about being short, and didn't believe her mother when she told her she would soon shoot up.

"What about you, Grace?" asked Maria.

"I'd like to invent a time machine," said Grace.

"Hey, that's cheating," said Kester. "You said to think of something useful!"

"It would be useful," said Maria. "You could go forward in time and find out the questions for a maths test."

"Or go back and change things," said Kester.

"Yes, you could go back and pick Paw-Paw up, so that he didn't trip Nana over," said Aimee.

They all agreed that the time machine would be the best invention of all. And since the other things would be just as difficult to invent, without being scientists and having laboratories, they all decided to concentrate on the time machine.

"Dials," said Raj. "You have to have dials and clocks and things."

"And wheels," said Grace.

"And maybe wings," said Maria.

Grace's back garden was soon so full of bits and pieces, it looked like a junkyard. There was an old radio that didn't work any more, two alarm clocks and Nana's kitchen timer, Grace's bicycle, five kitchen chairs and a big beach umbrella.

This time there was room for all five children and the thing they built really did look like a mad inventor's time-travelling machine. They had a wonderful afternoon travelling all over the world. (Grace's atlas was propped up on the bicycle handlebars, so that they could choose places as well as times.)

Kester chose to go into the future with Raj and Grace, Maria and Aimee all walked round with saucepans on their heads being future people.

Maria and Aimee went back to the dinosaurs and Raj was a Tyrannosaurus Rex, while Grace was a Triceratops and Kester a Stegosaur. There was so much roaring that Nana hobbled to the back door to see what was the matter. She shook her head when she saw the time machine.

Grace wanted to go sideways to Africa, with

Aimee and Kester. "That's not time travel," objected Raj.

"All right then," said Grace. "Make it last year when I went to The Gambia."

Aimee ran to fetch the crocodile again and Raj played the drums, while Maria danced what she thought might be an African dance.

"How lovely!" said Grace, stepping out of the time machine. "It is so hot here in Africa."

"Have some mango," said Maria. "And what else do you get in Africa?"

"Melon," said Grace, "and papaya and passion-fruit and jackfruit."

"Well, let's have those things too," said Maria.

"Let's give Nana a turn," said Aimee. "She could get into the time machine without any trouble."

So they went to fetch Nana and she carefully sat in one of the chairs, balancing her crutches against the bicycle.

"Choose a place," said Kester, showing her the atlas.

"Oh, no question," said Nana. "Trinidad, where I was born."

She found it on the map and showed it to them.

"And when would you like it to be?" asked Maria.

"Oh," said Nana, "when I was a little girl about your age. Let's say sixty years ago."

Maria adjusted the radio dial, set the two alarm clocks and made the kitchen timer ring.

"Let me help you out of the machine," said Grace. "You are now in Trinidad."

Nana was very used to playing Grace's games. She got out of the time machine and looked around her full of wonder, just like a little girl, even though she still had crutches.

"Oh, how wonderful!" she said, in a little girl's voice, pointing at the house with her crutch. "There's the house where I grew up. Can't you see the purple bougainvillea growing up the side of it? And over there is the path down to the beach where the fishermen catch crabs in their pots. I bet my brother Maxie is down there playing in the sand. And listen!I can hear my mother calling me ... Lucie ... Lucie!"

The children all listened. Nana made it all seem so real. Then they did hear the voice. "Lucie ... Lucie."

"The time machine!" gasped Grace. "It's

worked!"

Then they saw Mrs Myerson looking over the fence. She was calling Nana.

"Whatever is that?" she said, looking at the time machine.

"Hello, Gerda," said Nana in her ordinary voice. "It's a wonderful machine that can take you back to when you were small."

"Or into the future," said Kester, "if you prefer."

"Would you like a go, Mrs Myerson?" asked Raj.

"We could come and walk you round," said Grace, who knew that the old lady was scared of going out in the street. They all thought that she would say no, but Mrs Myerson did come and try the time machine.

She chose Germany as her place in the atlas, and 1925 as the year. Old Mrs Myerson looked very strange sitting upright in one of Grace's kitchen chairs, closing her eyes and muttering while Raj set the dials.

Then, when she opened her bright dark eyes, it was as if she couldn't see the children in the garden at all.

"Heidelberg," she whispered. "My grandparents' house with the big garden. They are all here, Mutti and Papa, my cousin Franz, my sister Hilde, my other cousins Fritz and Lili, oh and the dogs ... so many dogs. It is a summer day and we are playing in the brook at the bottom of the garden. Fritz is catching minnows and splashing my dress. Oh, and it's such a pretty dress – white with a blue sash."

The children all held their breath. Mrs Myerson had never told them anything about her family before. Now they were coming alive before their eyes.

"Hilde is picking flowers for the dinner table," went on Mrs Myerson. "Lilies and roses. Franz asks her for a rose for his buttonhole and she gives him a pink one with a heavenly scent. I can smell it now."

Suddenly she stopped, and the children saw she was crying. They felt terrible. But she wiped her eyes with a lacy handkerchief and said, "Thank you children. It is a wonderful machine."

"I think it's time to come back to the present and have a good strong cup of tea," said Nana.

But Mrs Myerson insisted on finishing the

game properly. She climbed back into the machine and had the dials re-set before she went into the kitchen with Nana.

"It's a miracle," Nana told Ma that evening. "Not only did Gerda Myerson walk round here from her house – she told us all about her childhood. She remembered how happy she was."

"It was just as if she really did travel back in time," said Grace.

"Then your machine works," said Ma. "What a wonderful invention!"

Starring Grace

The next post brought Grace an envelope with a crocodile stamp on it. It was her monthly letter from Africa, and it was satisfyingly fat. There was a letter from Papa, which she saved to read later, two chatty pages from Jatou, a note from Neneh and a picture from Bakary. It was a crayon drawing of an animal, which could have been anything, but Neneh had written 'Corned Beef' underneath, which was the name of their dog.

Grace pinned the picture to her noticeboard and put the letters from Jatou and Neneh in her stationery folder. Then she took Papa's letter out to the back garden, to read in her special place under the tree. It reminded her of the jackfruit tree in the backyard of Papa's compound in The Gambia, where she used to sit with him in the warm evenings when her little brother and sister had gone to bed.

The letter was a lovely one, full of details

about the family's life. Grace closed her eyes after she had read it and, with the sun on her face, imagined herself back in Bakau. She could almost smell the ocean.

A shadow fell across her face, blocking out the sun.

"A penny for your thoughts, Grace," said Nana.

"I was wishing my time-machine really worked," said Grace. "I went back to Africa in it, but it was only playing. I'm still here and Papa is miles away."

"You know what?" said Nana, settling down in her deckchair. "I think we all have a kind of time-machine in our heads. When I came out, I swear *you* were miles away. I bet you were in Africa with your papa."

"Yes, I was," said Grace, surprised. Then she looked sad again. "But it was only pretend."

"Pretending is making up things that haven't happened," said Nana. "What you were doing was remembering something that did happen. That's quite different. But pretending is good too and you are very good at it. Just think of all the pretending you have done this summer with your friends."

"Yes," said Grace. "We pretended a ghost and found Mrs Myerson. And we pretended a jungle and found a garden."

"I wonder whether you'd all like to do some more pretending," said Nana.

"What do you mean?" asked Grace.

"Well, my paper says the local theatre is putting on a musical and they're looking for some kids to be extras."

"A real show? In a real theatre?"

After that, there was no holding Grace. As soon as her friends came over, she showed them the advertisement in the paper. Kester and Aimee both wanted to go to the audition, but Maria and Raj weren't so sure.

"I'd rather watch," said Maria.

"I'd like to help with the lights," said Raj.

"Oh come on," said Grace. "It'll only be fun if we all do it."

So in the end they all did. They turned up at the theatre on Saturday afternoon and waited in line with a lot of other children of all ages and sizes. The musical was 'Annie' and the girl who was going to be Annie had already been chosen. She was much older than Grace and her friends –

in fact she was really fifteen – but she was small for her age and had been acting for years. Her name was Brianna and she was really friendly. She put on a bubbly red wig to show them.

"I'll have freckles too," she said, "when the make-up people have finished with me."

Grace was in her seventh heaven. She loved the smell of the theatre, and it had red plush tip-up seats like the ones in the theatre where Nana had once taken her to the ballet.

A busy lady with a clipboard took their names.

"Orphans on this side, street urchins over there," she said.

"I don't know if I'm an orphan or an urchin," whispered Kester.

"The orphans all have to be girls," said Grace, who knew the video and tape of 'Annie' by heart. "You'll have to be a street urchin."

"Then I'll be one too," said Raj.

So the two boys went over to the other side and Maria went with them.

"If I have to be in the play, I'm not going to be an orphan," she said. "Street urchins sound like more fun."

Grace and Aimee liked the idea of being

orphans, because they got to sing. First they watched all the boys and some girls being led across the stage, while the clipboard lady whispered to a bearded man sitting in a tip-up seat right in the middle of the theatre.

"He must be the director," whispered Grace.

Only about a quarter of the boys and girls were asked to stay. Kester, Maria and Raj were all chosen. Lots more girls wanted to be Annie's orphan friends, and they had to go up in batches while they were taught the tune and words of 'It's a hard knock life.' A lady with frizzy ginger hair and a big bosom played a piano at the side of the stage.

"I'm getting very tired of that song," said Ma to Nana.

"We knew it pretty well already, didn't we, Ava?" said Nana, winking at Grace.

But Grace wasn't tired of any of it. When it was her turn to go up on the stage with the other girls, she felt so excited she started to dance, even though they hadn't been taught any steps. She knew the words without looking at the blackboard. It was one of her favourite songs.

The clipboard lady called Grace and Aimee

over, and they were chosen too! Afterwards, the gang went back to Grace's house and talked excitedly in the garden. Maria and Raj had forgotten about not wanting to be in the play.

"It was so cool," said Maria, "being on stage in a proper theatre. Much better than the school hall."

"And we get to wear rags!" said Kester, with a big grin."We haven't got any words to learn, though," said Aimee, "apart from the songs."

"Good," said Raj. "It wouldn't be fun if we had to learn speeches."

But Grace wouldn't have minded learning speeches. She had a private dream that Brianna might get sick and then she, Grace, would step in to play her part, red wig and all. After all, she knew all the words.

Grace and Aimee didn't have named parts; none of the local children did. All the orphans who had things to say, like Molly, Pepper and July, were played by older girls like Brianna. But Grace and her friends had to go to just as many rehearsals as the main actors. Nana brought and collected them every day. Her leg was better now.

"This show has come along just in time," she told Grace. "You were all beginning to be bored with nothing to do but play."

It was true. The gang had just about thought of everything they could play that summer and there were still two weeks before they went back to school. 'Annie' was going to start in six weeks' time.

"All the kids who went to camp are going to be so sick," said Maria. "They didn't even get the chance to audition."

The days flew by. The orphans had song and dance routines to master, which they practised over and over again. And the street urchins had to learn movements that were just as complicated as dance steps. There were a lot of them and they had to be in their right places on stage at all times.

It was very tiring, but they had lots of breaks and drinks and chocolate biscuits. The actor playing Daddy Warbucks was a nice, funny man called Eric, with lots of brown hair, but he was going to wear a bald 'wig' for the performances. And there was going to be a real dog playing Sandy. He was specially trained, but he didn't come to the early rehearsals. Grace couldn't wait to see him; she loved dogs.

The children went back to school in the first week of September. Natalie had been to France and some of the children had been on even grander holidays. But no one was in the musical except for Grace and her friends.

"We should call ourselves the Annie Gang now," said Aimee.

The only thing Grace was sad about was that Papa would not be able to see her acting in a proper play. She wrote him a long letter all about it. And Ma promised to take photos and have two lots developed so that Grace could send one set to Papa.

Brianna stayed healthy. But on the day of the dress rehearsal, Lara, the girl playing July, came down with a bad attack of laryngitis. She couldn't speak at all! Daniel Laski, the bearded director, sent his assistant, Emma, the clipboard lady, to the crowded dressing-room. It was full of "orphans" having dirt-smudges carefully applied to their faces and their clean shiny hair mussed up with grey powder.

"Grace, can you come and speak to Daniel?" said Emma. Grace's heart started to pound. Perhaps he wanted her to be Annie after all! But he just asked if she knew the words July had to say.

"I've watched you during rehearsals," he said. "And I think you know all the parts."

Grace couldn't speak, but she nodded.

"Could you step in for Lara, just until she gets her voice back?" he asked. "You'd be doing us a big favour. Of course, you are very young to have a speaking part, so I'll quite understand if your parents don't want you to do it. We have to have their permission."

"I'll get my nana now," said Grace and rushed off to find her. But Nana wouldn't say yes straight away. "You know I'll have to ask your ma, Grace," she said.

Mr Laski said they could use the phone in his office. "I really need to get this sorted out as soon as possible," he said.

Nana rang Ma at the hospital. Grace anxiously watched Nana's face as she explained everything. "Hm, hm, uh-uh, right, yes, OK, I understand, yes, I'll tell him." And then Nana put the phone down. Grace was sure that Ma had said no.

"She says yes," said Nana, and Grace gave a

big squeal and danced Nana all around Mr Laski's office. He was laughing and trying to get out of their way.

"Here's the form for Grace's mother to sign," he said. "Bring it to the theatre tomorrow.

The next day was the big one. First night. The theatre was sold out. Grace peeped through a gap in the curtain and saw Ma and Nana sitting a few rows back. And there was Vincent, sitting beside Ma. "I might have known," she thought. And then she thought, "I'm glad he's here. I want everyone to see me."

Then she noticed someone else, next to Nana. It was Mrs Myerson! But there was no time to wonder about that; the orchestra players were coming into the pit and Emma shooed the children away from the curtain back to the dressing-rooms.

Grace wasn't in the big dressing-room with all the other orphans now. She was sharing a smaller one with the girls playing Molly and Duffy and Pepper. Brianna was in there too, putting on her wig. There was a knock at the door. It was Aimee.

"I came to say good luck, Grace," she said.

"Thank you," said Grace. She suddenly felt shy.

"What we say in the theatre is 'Break a leg'," said Brianna, laughing.

"I wouldn't dare say that anywhere near Grace," said Aimee.

Then it was time to go on. Grace had the time of her life. It was as good as being Peter Pan – better, in some ways. Because, although it wasn't the main part, it was in a real theatre, with real footlights and spotlights and a real red velvet curtain with gold braid and tassels.

When the show was over, and the cast had taken four curtain-calls, Ma and Nana and Vincent and Mrs Myerson came backstage to find Grace, and they all had flowers for her. Grace's arms were full of bouquets.

Then Ma gave her an extra one: "These came for you this afternoon." It was a bouquet of roses, and the card said,

For Grace, the famous actor,
from her loving Papa
and her African family.

For Grace, the
from her
and her African

Grace buried her face in all her flowers.

"It was only a small part," she said.

"Honey," said Ma, "as far as we are concerned, you were the star of the show."

"Yes," said Nana. "Whatever she does, Grace is always a star."

Mary Hoffman has written around 90 books for children and in 1998 was made an Honorary Fellow of the Library Association. She is also the editor of the children's journal *Armadillo*. In 1992 *Amazing Grace*, her first book for Frances Lincoln, was selected for Children's Books of the Year, commended for the Kate Greenaway Medal and included on the National Curriculum Reading List. It is an international bestseller and is now recognised as a classic picture book. *Amazing Grace* was followed by the picture books *Grace and Family* and *Princess Grace* and two other Grace storybooks – *Encore Grace!* and *Bravo, Grace!* Mary recently wrote the teenage Stravaganza trilogy and the historical novel *The Falconer's Knot*. *Kings and Queens of the Bible* is the latest of her Bible retellings, which include *Parables, Miracles* and *Animals of the Bible*.